A Giant First-Start® Reader

This easy reader contains only 53 different words,
repeated often to help the young reader develop
word recognition and interest in reading.

Basic word list for *Halloween Party*

a	games	party
and	go	Peter
are	good	play
be	Halloween	playing
beautiful	happy	princess
Billy	he	scary
cake	here	she
can	hooray	the
clown	how	then
come	is	there
comes	it	to
costume	Jenny	treat
costumes	let's	what
do	like	who
eat	monster	will
for	my	you
fun	now	your
funny	or	

Halloween Party

Written by Kathy Feczko

Illustrated by Blanche Sims

Troll Associates

Library of Congress Cataloging in Publication Data

Feczko, Kathy.
   Halloween party.

   Summary: The children have a wonderful time wearing
costumes and playing games at a Halloween party.
   1. Children's stories, American.   [1. Halloween—
Fiction.   2. Parties—Fiction]   I. Sims, Blanche, ill.
II. Title.
PZ7.F2985Hal   1985   [E]   84-8635
ISBN 0-8167-0354-X (lib. bdg.)

10   9   8   7   6   5   4

Let's go to a Halloween party.

What fun it will be! Hooray!

There will be costumes.

There will be games. Hooray!

There will be cake. *M-m-m, good!*

Will you come to my party?

Here comes a monster.

What a scary monster!

Who can he be?

Is it Billy?

Here comes a princess.

What a beautiful princess!

Who can she be?

Is it Jenny?

Here comes a clown.

What a funny clown! Hooray!

Who can he be?

Is it Peter?

What will you be for Halloween?

Will your costume be scary
or beautiful or funny?

Now Billy and Jenny and Peter
are playing games.

What fun the games are!

Here is a treat—a Halloween cake!

How good the cake is! *M-m-m, good!*

Do you like to play games?

Do you like to eat cake?

Then come to my party!

Happy Halloween!